Never give up on
abundantdreams.
Believe in all your
dreams.

Don Cates

Dedicated
to
my dear friend and brother firefighter
RUSS BONK
and to
the family of volunteer firefighters and
EMS personnel throughout the world.

Willy The Little Jeep Who Wanted To Be A Fire Truck

Copyright © 2003 by Donald M. Estes

THE ATTIC STUDIO Publishing House
P.O. Box 75 • Clinton Corners, NY 12514
Phone: 845-266-8100 • *Fax:* 845-266-5515
Willy's web site: www.willythejeep.com

PRINTED IN THE UNITED STATES OF AMERICA
10   9   8   7   6   5   4   3   2   1   FIRST EDITION

Library of Congress Cataloging-in-Publication Data

Estes, Don, 1953–
   Willy : the little jeep who wanted to be a fire truck / by Don Estes ; illustrated by Sue M. Garrison.—1st ed.
         p. cm.
Summary: Willy's lifelong dream of becoming a fire truck comes true and sends him on a journey from Clinton Corners, New York, to Clinton, Connecticut, and back home. Based on a true story.
   ISBN 1–883551–47–1 (alk. paper)
   [1. Automobiles—Fiction. 2. Fire engines—Fiction. 3. Parades—Fiction.]
   I. Garrison, Sue M., 1960– ill. II. Title.
PZ7.E7488Wi 2003
[Fic]—dc21
                                                    2003013023

Willy

THE LITTLE JEEP
WHO WANTED TO BE
A FIRE TRUCK

by **Don Estes**

Illustrated by **Sue M. Garrison**

The Attic Studio Press
CLINTON CORNERS, NEW YORK

Contents

WILLY HAD a good home and a family that loved and cared for him. He enjoyed helping with many chores—from carrying firewood to pulling large loads. But most of all, he enjoyed giving his family rides through the woods and into town.

During these rides, Willy often took his family to the firehouse. He loved to watch all the activity and see the shiny fire trucks.

One day Willy overheard one of the fire trucks say, "Here comes that little jeep again. Why should we talk to him? He doesn't have a siren, or hoses, or anything to help fight a fire. What good is he?"

This really hurt Willy, but he still looked forward to his visits to the firehouse.

FIREHOUSE

The fire trucks were big and bright and ready to race out of the firehouse at a moment's notice. But they wouldn't play or even talk to Willy—that is, all except one.

Big Blue didn't rush out of the firehouse when the siren screamed, but simply smiled as he watched the activity. Big Blue was not like the other fire trucks. He was older and, oddly enough, *blue.*

Big Blue had fought a lot of fires during his many years of active service. And now he had a special job—a very special job.

On parade days, Willy watched happily as all the volunteers washed Big Blue and put beautiful flags all over him. Then, when it was time for the parade, Big Blue was ready to go.

He would happily roll down the street with a cargo of smiling, waving children. People standing along the parade route would clap their hands, cheer, and wave back as Big Blue would pass by them.

Willy knew that he wanted to be a fire truck just like "Blue."

Even though he was afraid that his friend might laugh at him, Willy decided to share his dream with Blue.

"I really want to be a fire truck, just like you," Willy told him. Big Blue didn't laugh, but simply nodded with old fire truck wisdom.

But the years slowly passed, and Willy did not become a fire truck like Blue. In fact, he started feeling very tired and weak. His paint and his dreams both began to fade.

His visits to the firehouse were fewer and fewer. The trips and chores that he once loved became more and more difficult.

One day his family wanted to go for a ride with Willy. But he couldn't even find the energy to crawl out of his warm bed in the barn. Some days Willy didn't even want to wake up.

Early one morning, Willy heard the familiar rumble of Blue in the distance. The sound grew louder, until the rumble was right outside his barn.

Willy looked up hopefully. He tried to call out, but could only manage a faint whisper. As Blue and the firefighters roared past on their way to a parade, Willy wondered if it was all just a bad dream.

Soon he was sound asleep again.

The leaves turned golden and fell, the snow blew, the rains came, and the seasons changed. And still Willy slept. He slept for a long, long time.

ONE SPRING EVENING, while Willy was in a deep, deep sleep, he began to hear strange noises in his barn. As he sleepily opened his eyes, he saw his old friends opening large toolboxes, removing many shiny tools.

"What's going on?" Willy wondered. "What are they going to do to me?"

But he soon relaxed under the skillful touch of the people he loved and trusted. They were using their tools to help him get better. Willy calmly drifted in and out of sleep while they worked on him.

As the firefighters continued to work on Willy, they were very caring and gentle. They made sure not to hurt their little friend as they helped him.

Willy was examined from top to bottom, and his worn-out parts were replaced with new ones. Even his motor was slowly and carefully removed, and taken to a special repair shop.

Willy was a little nervous as he sleepily watched and waited. But he was also excited by all the attention. He wondered to himself, "What will I look like when they're done? Maybe like Blue!"

Time passed — and bolt by bolt, piece by piece, Willy slowly felt himself being put back together.

Willy started feeling better and younger than he had for a long time. Near the end of his operation, he was sprayed with a fresh coat of bright red paint.

"Oh well, at least it's the same color I was born with," Willy chuckled, "even if it's not blue!"

Willy purred happily when his family sat in his new seats and asked to go for a ride. He knew exactly where he was going to take them.

"I can't wait to see Blue!" Willy hummed. "I wonder if he'll remember me."

At first, his old friend did not recognize the bright red jeep. But when he did, Big Blue's springs squeaked with pure joy. Warm and happy memories flooded Willy's mind. He also remembered his old dream, and said, "I'm still not a fire truck like you, Blue."

Big Blue just nodded with old fire truck wisdom.

Willy still enjoyed watching the other fire trucks at the firehouse. He especially liked when they rushed out of the station with their sirens blaring and their lights flashing. He would get goosebumps every time the siren shouted.

Just as before, he looked on happily as Big Blue was washed and scrubbed for his parades. And Willy always jumped to help each time he was asked. Often, he'd run to the store for more soap and wax for Blue, as well as refreshments for the firefighters. But oh how he wanted to be a special fire truck like Big Blue.

ONE SUNNY DAY, the firehouse was buzzing with excitement. Big Blue and his friends had been invited to attend a special parade. It was so far away that they would be gone from home for the whole weekend!

Even though they tried to look their best, the firemen didn't invite the regular fire trucks to go. They would have to stay home to handle any fires that might happen.

But the firemen discovered that they had a real problem.

The fire company had older volunteers who would not be able to march the long parade route. Big Blue would be able to carry a few in his seat, but there still wasn't enough room for everyone who needed a ride. Suddenly, the talking stopped. The firemen all turned and looked at Willy.

At first, he felt embarrassed, wondering if he had spilled some oil or gas. But then he asked himself, "Are they looking to me to help solve their problem?"

Willy wondered how he could possibly help.

A week later, Willy drove his family to the firehouse. Something was very different about this night.

Willy went straight into the firehouse, right past the other fire trucks, and parked next to Big Blue. Many firefighters were standing around—as if they were waiting just for him.

The firefighters swarmed around Willy, holding fire hoses, nozzles, axes, coats, and helmets. They took  off Willy's hood, and all he could think to himself was, "Oh boy, here we go again!"

But this time, instead of taking him apart, the firemen spent hours carefully putting each piece in its specially chosen spot.

Willy was even given his own siren and red light, just like Big Blue's!

At the very end of the job, Willy's hood was placed back on — now decorated with the fire department sign, beautifully painted for all to see.

All the men and women of the fire department stood back, congratulated one another, and clapped their hands. Willy looked over at Big Blue and was surprised to see a tear rolling off one of his huge headlights. Blue was smiling. It was a tear of gladness and joy. Willy's friend once again nodded with old fire truck wisdom.

FIREHOUSE

Willy did not go home to his barn that night. Instead, he slept next to Blue in the firehouse, where all real fire trucks sleep.

The next evening, a huge truck that Willy had never met before came to the firehouse, pulling the largest trailer he had ever seen.

The firemen helped Willy and Big Blue on to the trailer.

They were carefully fastened down to be sure they did not roll off during the ride.

Willy was a little frightened, but he trusted his family and friends. And he noticed that even Blue looked a little nervous.

By then, it was very late at night. It was the first time either one had ever slept outside in their entire lives. Well, at least they tried to sleep. But thinking of their new adventure kept them both awake for hours. They spoke to each other in hushed tones, afraid to wake up the big truck. But he simply snored.

Early the next morning, the firemen returned to the station. They carefully checked the chains holding Blue and Willy safely on the huge trailer and woke up the big truck for the long trip.

There was a rumbling sound as the big truck woke up. Black smoke poured from his large smokestack.

Willy politely introduced himself to the truck. But the truck only grunted, "My name is Mac. Can't talk now. Got work to do. Got work to do. Got work to do."

Willy noticed the other fire trucks sitting in their house looking on as Mac prepared to leave. "I'm so happy the firemen asked me to help," thought Willy. "But the other fire trucks will *never* like me now!"

As Mac pulled away from the firehouse, Willy and Blue held on for dear life. They were carried over hills, down valleys, and through small towns. Cars passed by and tooted their horns while their passengers smiled and waved at Willy and Blue. People standing by the road cheered and waved as they went by. Mac blasted his mighty airhorn in reply.

They crossed a huge bridge and Willy, with his eyes mostly squinted shut, could still see great ships below him. One of the ships even blew her whistle at them. "This is the most fun I've ever had," thought Willy. But little did he know that the best was yet to come.

I T WAS LATE AFTERNOON by the time Mac pulled up to a big new firehouse.

"This is quite some place," said Blue.

"So big and beautiful," said Willy. "But I don't know anyone here."

Willy noticed that the firemen at the station were all staring at him. He felt embarrassed, not sure what to do or say.

"They seem to like little red fire trucks," Blue said smiling.

Big Blue and Willy were carefully unchained and rolled off the trailer. Willy tried to thank Mac for the nice ride, but he was already sound asleep.

Big Blue immediately rolled into the new firehouse as if he lived there and started to make new friends. He was happy to spend the night there.

But Willy felt better staying with his own family. He drove them to a big campground and was glad to see many of his friends from home already there. Willy especially enjoyed helping them set up camp for the night.

There was much talk and excitement in the air about the next day's special parade. To be sure they all got a good night's sleep for the big event, everyone went to bed early. But Willy stayed awake for a long time, sitting by the campfire and gazing at the moon and stars.

The next morning, Willy took time to give all his friends and their children rides around the campground. They all played together until it was time to get ready for the big parade.

Suddenly there was a rumbling sound as Blue thundered into the campground. "This is your big day little buddy," he said.

The firemen started scrubbing Willy and Blue. Once they had gotten them all bright and shiny, they placed new flags on both of them. Willy was ready. The firemen put on their neatly pressed uniforms, and the marching band arrived.

Everyone climbed on Willy and Big Blue for a ride into town where the parade was about to begin. Willy had never seen so many fire trucks or people in his life.

As they all waited their turn in the parade, the band tuned up, and everyone took pictures. When it was his turn to go, Willy froze in place. He was afraid that he might make a mistake and people would laugh at him. But Blue was there to encourage him and calm his fears. The band played, the firefighters marched, and on they went.

Willy had watched many parades in the past, but nothing was quite like this. There were hundreds of people lining the streets, and they all seemed to be cheering just for him.

Many people took pictures of the little red fire truck and his passengers as they went by. Willy puffed himself up as big as possible, trying to look as much like Big Blue as he could. People stood up and clapped, and some even saluted.

"This is what I've always wanted," said Willy.

"Yes, it is," thundered Blue. The parade went on and on, but for Willy, it was over all too soon. Willy felt overjoyed from the experience.

After the parade was over, there was a big carnival. Willy and Big Blue sat outside and watched as their fire friends laughed and enjoyed themselves at the celebration. There was music and dancing. Willy and Blue tried to hum along, but they weren't familiar with any of the songs.

Many people in the crowd began to gather close to the stage, where there were rows and rows of big sparkling trophies lined up on a table.

"Oh, wouldn't it be great if we could get one of those trophies to take home?" Willy said to Big Blue. Blue just nodded with old fire truck wisdom.

There was loud cheering, and Willy could just barely see some of his friends through the crowd. He caught a glimpse of a friend going up on the stage to carry off one of the sparkling trophies, lifting it high in the air.

This happened several times, until one trophy stood alone, unclaimed. It was the most beautiful of them all.

An announcement came over the loudspeaker that this final trophy was for the fire company with the best spirit and teamwork.

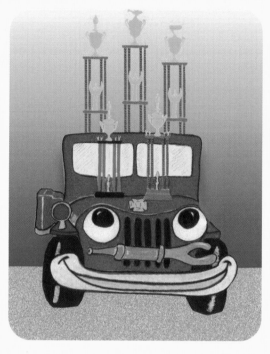

To Willy's surprise, all of his firefighter friends jumped up on the stage and carried off this very special prize. It was the tallest trophy of all.

Soon Willy's friends came out of the carnival grounds carrying one trophy after another to show Willy and Blue.

The firemen all cheered again and climbed up on Big Blue and Willy for a ride back to the campground. Willy's friends were as happy as he had ever seen them. He himself was happier and prouder than he had ever been in his entire life.

When they got back to the campground, other campers and the friendly park rangers came around to see what the noise was all about. Willy proudly held the trophies on his hood for everyone to see and admire.

After their friends made a big campfire, Willy and Blue gathered close to enjoy the warmth of the fire and their friendship. When everyone had gone to bed, the two of them stayed by the fire. They watched the stars and listened to the rolling waves on the nearby beach.

Before he drifted off to sleep, Willy's last thought was, "I am finally a real fire truck."

That night, he slept better than he ever had before.

*T*HE NEXT MORNING Willy's friends packed up for the long trip home. Mac and his huge trailer came rumbling over for his load of the big and little fire trucks. He looked at Big Blue and then Willy. "Nice job, guys," he said with a grin. "Now get on. Got work to do. Got work to do. Got work to do."

Big Blue and Willy were again safely chained on the big trailer. Willy was not as nervous as he had been the first time.

Much to Willy's surprise, one of the firemen lifted up the biggest trophy of all and placed it carefully on Willy's front seat. He tied it in to be sure that Willy did not accidentally drop it.

The long ride home didn't seem quite as exciting as the ride on the way out. Big Blue dozed most of the way, but Willy could not keep from smiling from headlight to headlight. They were carried through small towns, down valleys, and over hills. When cars tooted and people waved, Willy held up his big trophy for all to see — and nodded with old fire truck wisdom, just as he had seen Big Blue do so many times before.

Mac rumbled through the countryside and, as time passed, the scenery began to look more and more familiar to Willy. He glanced over as Blue gave a grand yawn and stretched high on his springs. Soon the drone of Mac's mighty motor changed pitch, and they began the descent into the little town that Willy and Blue called home.

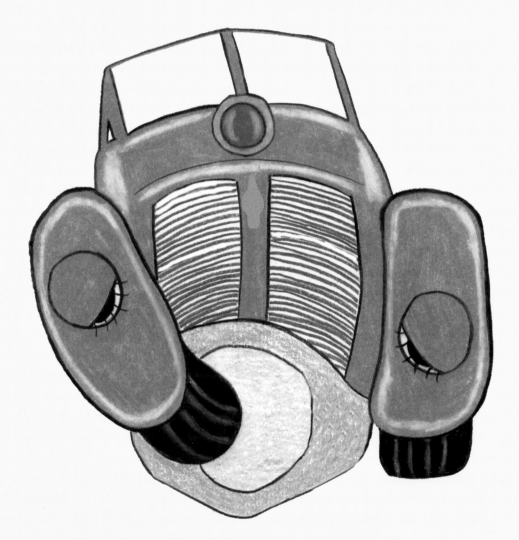

Willy soon saw buildings that he knew, and within minutes Mac groaned to a stop at their firehouse.

Willy had only been away for a short time, but the comforting sights of his hometown made him feel warm and happy. He was glad to see that all of his fire friends were also safely back at home after the long trip, waiting to help Big Blue and him off the huge trailer.

"Well, Blue," said Willy, "I guess I can go back to my barn now and catch up on some sleep." It was Big Blue's turn to nod with old fire truck wisdom.

Just as Blue and Willy were safely helped down and were firmly on the ground once again, all the firehouse doors were opened wide, and the siren began to scream.

Strangely, the other fire trucks did not race from their beds. Instead, they slowly crept forward. Willy, confused and a little frightened, moved back to make sure he was not in the way. But Blue held his ground. In fact, he gently nudged Willy forward. Then all the firemen lined up just as they had for the big parade. They were not wearing their neatly pressed uniforms, and there was no band. But it seemed to Willy that they were going to have a parade just the same.

All the other sparkling trophies were placed on Willy's seats, and before he knew what was happening, Blue nudged him again to the front of everyone. The other fire trucks fell in line behind Willy and Blue. And they all marched up the road and into town.

"That's strange," thought Willy. "The big fire trucks are smiling at me. And they even let me go first!"

People from the town began to come out of their houses to see what all the noise was about. Soon more and more of the town folks were standing on their porches, clapping and cheering.

By the time the small parade had turned around and headed back towards the firehouse, nearly everybody in town had come outside to join in the cheering and waving. Some even fell in line with the parade.

There were not nearly as many people watching as there had been in the big parade, but Willy felt even more proud, knowing that these were his hometown friends and neighbors.

Willy suddenly realized that in all his desire to be a fire truck and with all the success of the big parade, this was where he belonged.

The people he knew were proud not just of him, but of the entire fire company and what they had done as a team. The trophies did not belong to Willy, or Blue, or even the fire company. They belonged to the people of the town who loved him and whom he loved in return.

When they got back to the firehouse, the fire trucks who had been so unfriendly before each drove by Willy and gave him a wink and a smile. It was his turn to have a tear of joy roll off his headlight.

The beautiful trophies were carefully placed in a special cabinet for everyone to enjoy.

Willy, now totally exhausted, brought his family back home.

His barn was a welcome sight. And though he had enjoyed his adventure more than anything he had done before, he found that the simple comfort of home and family gave him a very special warmth inside.

After he was snuggled in for the evening, Willy thought about all that had happened and how much he had grown up in a short time. He also wondered what adventures tomorrow would bring.

Soon, Willy dozed off to sleep, dreaming the dreams of a little red fire truck.

The End

A NOTE
from WILLY

HELLO, I'M WILLY. (See my license plate?) Did you know that the story in this book really happened?

I still live with my family near the firehouse in Clinton Corners, New York, where so much of the story takes place.

I hope you enjoyed reading about my friends and the fun we had during our special adventures. We travelled more than 100 miles from our hometown to be part of that beautiful parade in Clinton, Connecticut.

Believe it or not, I was born in 1947. For quite a while now, I've lived in Clinton Corners, where I was adopted by my family many years ago.

My best friend, Big Blue, lives down the road from me. He is a very special 1941 American LaFrance fire truck. Ol' Blue has had only one home in his life: with the Clinton Volunteer Fire Department (CVFD). They like to call him "Bluebird."

— OVER —

All the people in my family are members of our local fire department. We spend a great deal of time at the firehouse where Blue lives. In the years ahead, I hope to be in a lot of parades. "Time will tell," as my Pop always says.

As you saw in my story, things don't always go according to your hopes and plans—not right away at least. During those hard times when I was feeling really tired and discouraged, I almost gave up on my dreams. But I learned to trust in others, and my dreams stayed alive. Remember the part of the story about my operation? It was a little scary at first. But I sure did like being made like new again. It was like getting all better after a bad cold. All I can say is: keep hoping and praying, never let go of your dreams, and things have a way of working out. Well, I need to run along now. I can't wait to see what my next adventure might be! Keep dreaming.

Your friend,

Willy

P.S. I hope someday to see you on the road, or during a school visit, or at a parade. In the meantime, please feel free to write me a letter: WILLY P.O. Box 7 Clinton Corners, NY 12514 or send me an E-mail note: Willy@willythejeep.com.

THANK YOU.

About the Author

DON ESTES *(a.k.a. "Willy's Pop")* has been a volunteer firefighter for nearly thirty years in Clinton Corners, New York. His talent for storytelling and his love of children led naturally to writing **Willy** for a friend and his family. The story is based on actual events in the towns of Clinton, New York and Clinton, Connecticut in which Don's fire company participated. Don's "day job" is as department administrator for emergency services at IBM in Poughkeepsie.

In recognition of his lifelong dedication to his hometown, Don Estes has been honored with several community awards for outstanding volunteer service. He has also served as Fire Chief of the East Clinton Fire District. His commitment to community service is shared by his wife, Lynn, and their children Matt and Amy, all members of the Clinton Volunteer Fire Department.

About the Illustrator

SUE M. GARRISON has been drawing since early childhood. She currently works as production supervisor in a technology firm in the Hudson Valley. For years, Sue's artwork has appeared on airbrushed shirts and hats. She currently lives in Dutchess County with her husband Chris and their Labrador retriever "Moose." For recreation, the Garrisons enjoy cruising on the Hudson River in their boat, *Second Wind.*

A Note of Thanks from Willy's Pop

THERE ARE MANY WONDERFUL PEOPLE who have dedicated a great deal of time and effort to help make the "Willy ride" a memorable adventure through the hills and valleys we've traveled together. Before proceeding to our long and cherished list of Willy elves on the next two pages, I first extend my most sincere gratitude to my dear friends and teammates: illustrator Sue Garrison, and publisher *(and chief editor and bottle-washer)* Joseph "Trip" Sinnott.

Sue, with the constant support of her husband Chris, poured herself into creating, modifying and polishing the lovable characters contained in this book. Her extraordinary effort has been a wonderful inspiration. For this and for her friendship, I shall be forever in her debt.

Trip goes far beyond the call of duty in his remarkable publishing efforts. I can never express all that he has done, but his renewed friendship *(catching up in our hometown after more post–Little League years than I care to count)* is perhaps the greatest gift from this incredible publishing experience.

May God bless you, Sue and Trip. And may God bless you, dear reader.

– DON ESTES

Acknowledgements & Credits

FROM THE AUTHOR
with special thanks to:

My wife Lynn for believing in me and supporting the project.

My mother Ruth (Raru) for being a great support and sounding board.

My children, Matt and Amy, for enduring the Willy marathon.

Russ Bonk for being my friend and right hand in the parade and for making Willy a fire truck

Russ's wife Stephanie and the Bonk children for their love of Willy.

My brother Tom, for his many hours of skilled mechanical labors on Willy.

My sister Nancy, for outfitting Willy with newly upholstered seats for the journey.

My extended family at the Clinton Volunteer Fire Department (NY).

The Clinton Fire Dept. (CT) for being such gracious hosts and friends.

FROM THE PUBLISHER
with special thanks to:

Sally Sinnott Guernsey for her enthusiasm for Willy and her love along the journey.

Illustrator Sue Garrison for her remarkable role in bringing Willy and his friends to life.

Chris Garrison for providing steadfast support to his wife Sue and gracious assistance during the Willy marathon.

Fred Feldman for bringing his 33 years of teaching wisdom to the Willy ride.

Sarah Sinnott for her timely hands-on support in the crunch time.

The Angell Family for their thoughtful reflections and insightful reviews.

Irene Decker for her invaluable help through all the many pre-press phases of Willy.

Eric Glass for his artistry, enhancing these pages with his colorful "landscaping" and lively "parade folk."